Living Rough

Living Rough

Cristy Watson

orca currents

ORCA BOOK PUBLISHERS

Library and Archives Canada Cataloguing in Publication

Watson, Cristy, 1964-
Living rough / Cristy Watson.
(Orca currents)

Issued also in electronic formats.
ISBN 978-1-55469-888-2 (bound).--ISBN 978-1-55469-434-1 (pbk.)

I. Title. II. Series: Orca currents
PS8645.A8625L59 2011   JC813'.6   C2011-903417-4

First published in the United States, 2011
Library of Congress Control Number: 2011929386

Summary: Poe, a homeless young teen, struggles to
keep his living situation a secret.

*Orca Book Publishers is dedicated to preserving the environment and has printed this
book on paper certified by the Forest Stewardship Council®.*

Orca Book Publishers gratefully acknowledges the support for its
publishing programs provided by the following agencies: the Government
of Canada through the Canada Book Fund and the Canada Council for the Arts,
and the Province of British Columbia through the BC Arts Council
and the Book Publishing Tax Credit.

Cover photography by iStockphoto.com
Author photo by Lynne Woodley

ORCA BOOK PUBLISHERS
PO Box 5626, Stn. B
Victoria, BC Canada
V8R 6S4

ORCA BOOK PUBLISHERS
PO Box 468
Custer, WA USA
98240-0468

www.orcabook.com
Printed and bound in Canada.

14 13 12 11 • 4 3 2 1

This book is dedicated to all the students with whom I've worked. Your resilience and constant hope inspire my characters. This book is also dedicated to a fabulous man we miss and love, Uncle George (1950–2011).

Chapter One

I didn't need a weatherman to tell me what to expect when I woke up. It was painfully clear. Well, the skies weren't clear. What *was* clear was that it was going to be another crappy day. How can it rain for twenty days straight?

I'd scrubbed last night, so I pulled my pants and shirt on. My clothes smelled musty and felt damp. I figured some fresh air would help, and I wanted to break my record for speed-walking to school. My best time was eighteen minutes. Rain is a good motivator for speed. So I grabbed my felt hat and headed out into the cool wet morning.

I wolfed down a granola bar as I started up the hill. I'd grabbed it from the breakfast program at school. No one wanted to call it what it was, a meal program for loser poor kids. I always arrived early so I could raid the food and clear out before the halls got busy.

But the risk of going *that* early was that I was usually the only kid in the joint, and the staff would try to have a heart-to-heart with me. Every day. Like my life changed between Monday and Tuesday. I'm only fifteen, after all.

I wasn't in the mood for conversation, so I was happy to find the room was empty. I figured it was safe to slip in and grab an apple from the food table. Sour juice ran down my chin as I bit into the green fruit. I'd just pocketed a peanut-butter granola bar when I heard voices. That was my cue to clear out of there.

I met one of the ladies that supervise the room on her way in. "Hi, Edgar," she said. "I thought you might like this raincoat." She held out a fluorescent blue jacket.

I shook my head and bolted down the hall. Couldn't she see I was a trench-coat kind of guy? As I rounded the corner by the library, I bumped into our principal.

"Mr. Reed," he said. He had a habit of calling students by their last name. I had often thought of calling him Pete to be funny, but I never quite got the courage.

"Hi, Mr. Johnson."

"Listen, I'm glad I ran into you," he continued. "I was wondering if you could do the school a favor."

I don't know why he talked about the school like it was a person.

"Could you show a new student around before the first bell? She arrived yesterday from the Ukraine and doesn't speak much English."

"I guess." I tried to sound non-committal. Maybe he'd come to his senses and find a keener, like someone from student council. But he didn't notice my lack of enthusiasm. He gestured for me to follow him toward the office.

As I walked behind Mr. Johnson, I counted the tiles on the floor. There were forty-one linoleum squares from the breakfast room to the office. Counting helped my nerves to chill.

"Inna, please meet Mr. Reed," said Mr. Johnson as he reached the foyer.

I couldn't believe he'd used her first name. Her last name must be a beast to pronounce. I kept my gaze toward the floor while I thought about how I could get out of this.

A hand came into my view. The nails were spattered with green polish and were bitten to the quick. This girl was a chewer. Maybe she'd be all right. I risked looking up at her.

"Hallo. I'm Inna," she said. Her accent was as thick as the mascara she'd darkened her lashes with. Eyeliner brightened her hazel eyes. Her lower lip quivered. She was obviously scared to death.

I'd be traumatized, too, if I didn't know the language. "I'm Edgar," I said as I shook her hand. I knew how to be polite. She smiled with what looked like relief. She didn't want to take the tour any more than I wanted to give it. Mr. Johnson was already retreating down the hall.

"Thank you, Mr. Reed. Welcome, Inna. Enjoy your day at Crescent High," he called over his shoulder.

"You're...welcome," she answered.

I smiled.

"Well, this is the office. Come here when you need to use the phone." I gestured making a phone call, and she smiled again. We headed in the direction Mr. Johnson had disappeared. The hall started to fill with students. As usual, most of them seemed intent on staring. I was used to the looks. I'm not sure how Inna was handling their glares.

Two girls from grade nine whispered and giggled as they looked our way. I moved toward them, giving them a dirty look. Before I said anything, they clammed up and took off.

"Tsank you," said Inna.

"Hey, no problem," I replied as I stopped by the orange doors at the end of the hall. "This is the gym. Place for exercise." I did two jumping jacks. Inna seemed to understand. Next stop would be the cafeteria, and then I'd need to help her find her class.

"Poe. Whaz up?" My only friend sauntered toward us. A book spilled from the pile in his arms onto the floor. Inna picked it up and passed it back to him. He gave her a goofy grin.

I looked Inna over again. She *was* kind of pretty. As she turned my way, I felt my cheeks get warm. I looked back at my buddy and sputtered, "Ben, meet Inna. Inna, Ben."

"I like your name," Ben said. "It's cool. How come I haven't seen you around before? Whose classes are you in? Are you in our grade?"

Ben was stringing the sentences together too fast for her to keep up. He probably lost her at *I like…*

"Whoa! Slow down," I said. Ben looked at me then back at her.

Inna scrunched up her eyebrows and seemed to be trying to piece together a response. "Grade? Ah…grade…ten," she finally answered. Maybe she knew more English than I realized.

As we headed toward the cafeteria, Ben followed a few paces behind, checking out her skirt. He gave me a thumbs-up out of Inna's range of vision.

"This is the cafeteria, but the food is bad." I plugged my nose.

"You giving a tour?" Ben asked.

"Yeah. Johnson cornered me. What could I do?"

"Told ya you should come to my place before school. You get here too early. I'd say, 'That'll teach you,' but this time you lucked out." Ben chuckled as he headed to his locker.

It was nearly time for the bell. "Can I see your schedule?" I asked Inna. She looked confused. I pointed at the paper in her hand. She passed it to me, and I scanned the sheet.

Her first block was English in room 203. My class was across the hall, so that made it easy. I could meet her at the bell to escort her to her second block. That's when she had science in the lab downstairs. *Poor girl. She'll never know what hit her.* Science is okay, but Mr. Rich has no idea how to teach teens. Frogs he gets—students make no sense to him.

Before lunch, Inna's class would be gym. It seemed straightforward enough. I could handle helping her get to her classes.

As the bell rang, a look of terror came over Inna's face. She bolted toward the office.

In seconds she was lost in a sea of students.

Chapter Two

"Inna!" I shouted over the bustle of people slamming lockers and hustling through the corridor. Usually I was in class by now. I hate halls. I hate crowds. And the crowds hate me.

"Hey, loser," said Theo, a grade twelve I always avoided. "Who let you out? Cave dweller."

I wanted to tell him he wasn't very original, but I was too busy trying to spot Inna. I kept walking.

"I'm talking to you, loser. Didn't you hear me?" he said, pushing me against a locker. I guess that was for effect. By now his buddies had shown up. I didn't stand a chance against that many of them.

Theo pushed my left shoulder, and I fell back into the locker again. I tried eye contact. He grabbed my chin and shoved me back so hard, I think my head left a dent in the metal door.

"Get him, dude," said one of his groupies.

Like he didn't already have me.

"What's going on here, gentlemen?" Mr. Johnson arrived on the scene. I would have chosen a different word than gentlemen.

"Ah, nothing, Mr. J. We were just asking Mr. Reed here to move away from our lockers. Don't want to be late for class, you know?"

"Well, get your things and move on." Mr. Johnson winked at me. He knew what was really going on. If he gave them heck, they would retaliate later. This way, I saved face and no one got hurt. I squeezed by one of the other kids and took off down the hall.

I felt the residue from their insults but brushed them away as I continued searching for Inna. Thankfully she was waiting outside the office, looking more embarrassed than afraid.

"I...sorry," she said.

"No problem. Come with me." The halls were nearly empty now. Only a few late students straggled to their rooms. We walked up the stairs and stopped outside her English class. The door was closed.

"This is your room," I said.

"Tsank you."

"At the end of class...wait here."
I pointed to an open space in the hall.
"I will get you...here." I pointed again,
and she nodded. I hoped she knew what
I meant.

I knocked on the door. Ms. Carfax
opened it and gestured for Inna to enter
the room. I could hear her telling the
class that Inna spoke little English. As
I turned to leave, I caught Inna looking
back at me and smiling. I felt an energy
surge through me. I couldn't wait for the
end of class so I could see her again.

I was usually careful *not* to let
anyone get under my skin.

What is it about her?

As I opened the door to social
studies, Mr. Brock gave me the evil
eye but didn't send me for a late slip.
Paul, another troublemaker (the school's
not short on them), tried to trip me as
I passed him. Their games were so old.
They'd been doing this since I arrived

last fall. I ignored Paul and slipped into my desk.

Seventy-two drops of rain slid down the window while Mr. Brock told us what we'd be studying next. I only half listened. I never sweated much because I usually got decent grades. And that's good. Even though it's a long shot, I hope to enroll at university when I finish high school. I'm not sure what I'll take, but I know I don't want to end up like my dad.

Mr. Brock mentioned an article he wanted to share with us, and I was brought back to reality. Something he said made me panic. I looked up. He was staring straight at me.

Did he know my secret?

Chapter Three

Mr. Brock asked us to turn to page seventy-two. He opened a newspaper story on the computer and projected the image onto the screen. My palms were sweating, and the pages of my textbook stuck to my fingers. This was going to be tricky. A few kids were looking at me.

Why are they staring?

Do they know?

Mr. Brock tapped my shoulder. I nearly jumped out of my seat.

"You're being paged, Edgar. One of your classmates can help you to catch up when you return."

Jeez, I hadn't even heard the announcement. I'm glad I didn't blurt anything out.

As I moved down the hall, I wondered who I needed to thank for the getaway?

For a moment, I considered returning to class to grab my books. Then I could bail on socials. But I figured Mr. Brock would wonder why I was back so quickly. So I headed toward the office, where I found Inna waiting for me.

"What's wrong?" I asked.

"Go home…I go home."

"You have to go home? But school isn't over…"

"Her parents are here. They have to sign some paperwork, and Inna needs to be with them." The secretary pointed to the door leading outside. I could see a silver Buick waiting with its engine running.

"I tell you I go home. Tsank you for today." Inna smiled. Her eyes danced like they were smiling too.

I couldn't believe what I was thinking. *Eyes dancing*…where did that come from?

But her eyes had this warmth that drew you into them. It was almost hypnotic. "Can I see you tomorrow? I mean, can I *help* you tomorrow?"

"Tomorrow. I…here…meet…here?" she asked.

"Yes. I will be here tomorrow. Good luck," I said as she turned toward the door. I let out the breath I'd been holding as I watched her car pull away from the school.

Mrs. Norris looked at me strangely. I realized my mouth was hanging open.

My insides felt strange. I couldn't get the image of Inna's smile out of my mind. I never bothered with girls. Most of them were too busy with gossip to notice anyone but their little groupies. And the rest were so preoccupied with how they looked that I wouldn't be included in their busy schedule of self-adoration anyway.

So why this girl?

"Mr. Reed."

"Mr. Johnson," I answered as I turned to face his six feet of principalship.

"Thank you for helping our new student today. I understand you were called down to speak with her again?"

"Yeah…Yes. She was picked up by her parents and wanted to let me know. So I wouldn't wait at her class."

"Well, your help has been noted. I also wanted to make sure you're aware that if you need to talk with someone, Mrs. Bailey is always available."

"Thanks." I loved how he slid out of actually helping me. As principals go, he's not that bad. He was pretty cool earlier, but when it came to what a student was struggling with, well, he left that to the counselors.

"You check in with Mrs. Bailey, okay?" He moved off in the direction of the gym, where I could hear a scuffle in the hallway.

I wasn't worried that Mr. J. knew what was *really* going on—he wasn't too good at noticing the signs. His comments were probably about the bullying he saw today. But still... I needed to take some extra precautions.

Chapter Four

Thankfully, with Mr. J.'s chat and a *loooong* walk back to class, I managed to return minutes before the bell. Mr. Brock gave us four pages to read for homework and sixteen questions to answer, then let us talk among ourselves until the bell rang.

"Hey, Poe, where's the new girl?" Ben asked during math.

"She took off for the rest of the day. Wish I had a reason to leave."

"I don't mind staying for drama class, but I'd rather be *anywhere* else than here." Ben continued, "Inna sure is pretty. Need an extra hand with her?" He ran his fingers through his mop of brown hair. Ben didn't have a way with the girls either. That was part of why we were friends. The main reason, though, was that we both like reading. These days book readers are rare—especially ones who read classics.

That's why Ben gave me the nickname Poe. My dad loved the guy's writing and named me Edgar Allan, but he never used the nickname. Ben thought I was lucky to be named after a writer like Edgar Allan Poe. His favorite story is *The Tell-Tale Heart*. I like *The Masque of the Red Death*. I bet Stephen King read all of Poe's works when he was growing up.

As our math teacher wrote a quadratic formula on the board, Ben sighed. He's not a numbers guy. Numbers stress him out. Ben shuffled through his backpack, pulling out papers and pencils and an old cookie that had a few bites out of it. He finished it off and rummaged in his pack again. This time he pulled out a graphic novel. He held it out of our teacher's sight and read while Mr. Pender continued with the lesson.

After distracting himself for the first half of the class, Ben leaned over and whispered, "I don't know how this stuff is going to make me a better actor. Shouldn't it be enough that I know how to keep track of my huge earnings once I'm a movie star?"

"I guess, but…"

He cut me off. "Isn't that what calculators are for?"

I smiled. He had a point.

For the rest of the period he let me help him with the equations. When the bell rang, we still had five questions to finish.

"Guess this will be for homework," said Ben. "Any chance you can—"

"Give you a hand?" I finished for him. "No problem."

After class, Ben wanted to grab lunch at the Happy Mart Food & Gas. They had a self-serve coffee bar in the store, and their Grin and Win contest was on. A happy face always adorned their cups during the contest. The tongue became a pull-tab that you peeled to reveal prizes, like $1000. I didn't have much cash, but what money I had, I used to buy coffee. I hoped to win something in the contest. I was aiming for the car, but even the $100 gift card would be all right.

As we approached the entrance, some guy nearly took us both out as he squeezed his Mercedes into the No Parking spot. He pushed through the door without holding it for us.

I stood by Ben at the cooler while he decided what he wanted. In the mirror above us, I could see the guy fixing his beverage at the coffee station. He placed two extra Grin and Win cups under the one he already had.

"What a creep," I said loudly. I glanced at the cashier.

She eyed me suspiciously. I wanted to say, *Save that look for him!* I nodded toward the guy, hoping she'd catch my drift. But she shook her head at me, like *I* was a loser, and then went back to reading her paper.

As I poured my coffee, I realized there weren't many prize cups left. The contest was nearly over. I could take extras too. My dad and I really needed the cash. I didn't think Mr. Mercedes was that desperate. But I knew it was wrong to take more than I'd paid for, and I didn't want to throw off my karma.

As the Mercedes driver left the store, I yelled, "Next time use a sleeve, buddy!"

He slid into his vehicle and slithered out of the parking lot.

"What was that about?" asked Ben as we left the store.

"Nothing, just another privileged *jerk* that doesn't know how to appreciate it."

"Sometimes, Poe, I think I should call you Mr. Philosopher."

I didn't answer. I felt riled up. Thinking about how hard this winter had been for my dad and me made my temples burn. Images of cold nights and hunger blurred my thoughts. I pushed them aside by counting one, two, three…986 steps back to school.

I finished my coffee as we reached the north doors. Several students were hanging around the entrance. "Let's chill a minute. Wait for the bell."

"Right," said Ben. He moved over to the wall, away from the group. "I have English next. We just started our Shakespeare unit."

"Which play are you doing?" I asked.

"*Macbeth*," he replied, pulling his collar up to keep his neck warm. "It had this awesome scene with witches."

"Right on," I said. "In my old school we read *Something Wicked This Way Comes* by Ray Bradbury. Pretty cool stuff with a witch in that book too."

"Hey, that title comes from a line in *Macbeth*." Ben's eyes wandered to three girls near the door. His cheeks flushed as one of them looked his way. "Maybe Saturday we could find movie versions of both? We can hang at my place and see if my folks will order us a pizza?"

I nodded as the bell rang. Before heading for our separate classes, we agreed to meet after school to do our homework together.

Chapter Five

The whole time we worked on our math at the coffee shop, trucks passed by and distracted me. Some were filled with dirt. Others had tree trunks and branches loaded in the back. It looked like heavy-duty clearing was going on nearby. Not that I'm surprised. It seemed like the trees on every patch of land disappeared in the blink of an eye.

As long as the trees around my place stayed put.

"So what do you think it's like in the Ukraine?" asked Ben, slurping his drink.

"I dunno. I wonder what made Inna's family move here," I said. I watched a kid from our school take a bite out of a sandwich. My stomach growled.

Ben followed my gaze. "Hey, I'm still hungry," he said. Wanna share a sandwich with me?"

"Naw…that's okay."

"Dude, I'm really craving one, but if I eat it all, I won't have room for supper. Then my mom'll get after me, for sure." He headed toward the counter to order.

I have to admit, the sandwich filled a void that was getting bigger and bigger every day.

I tested Ben with questions from our lessons. "Think you're ready for the exam?" I asked after I'd been quizzing him for twenty minutes.

"Yeah. No...I guess." We laughed. I thanked Ben for the food, then started home.

Twenty-six suvs passed me before I reached our place.

As I rounded a curve in the road, the air was sucked from my lungs. What I saw totally caught me off guard. I swallowed and took a deep breath.

The trucks I'd seen from the coffee shop must have come from here.

I stared at a gaping hole that had been a forest this morning. Now bulldozers pushed dirt into piles. Trees were ripped right out of the ground. Men in hard hats stood around talking and pointing.

There'd been no warning this was coming.

A hand on my shoulder made me jump.

"Easy, kid. It's just me." My dad climbed off his bike. He put his hands over his eyes to block out the sun as he surveyed the devastation.

Even though the rain had stopped, I felt as though I needed to find shelter.

"When did this start, Dad?"

"After you left for school. I don't know what time, but it was definitely early. Made an awful lot of noise." My dad shook his head. "You hungry?" he asked.

"Naw. Ben and I shared a sandwich. How about you?"

"Oh, I had a fabulous lunch," answered my dad.

He probably hadn't eaten.

"Since there was such a racket going on here," he continued, "I headed over to the library. I got a couple of books you might like."

"Thanks," I said. "I'll check them out after I finish up my homework." I left my dad surveying the damage.

When I got settled in, I found it tough to concentrate on my social studies assignment. The subject matter was heavy-duty. And my mind wandered to the problem of the trees being cleared so near our place. I felt the beginnings of a headache, so I decided to go for a walk. I was just heading out when my dad came in.

"Leaving so soon? I thought we could play cards or something."

"Cards?" I felt my temples squeeze together, like Theo had my head in a vise grip. My dad had this delusion that things were all right. He thought that if we acted as if everything was normal, it wouldn't matter where we were. I didn't have the energy to argue with him, so I agreed to keep him company.

We played three games of cribbage. Dad won every game by a mile. I pegged lots, but that was it. When we tallied our hands at the end of each round, I mostly had nothing that counted for points. My dad had the knack for getting jacks and fives...together. He may not have been lucky in life, but he sure had good luck with cards.

As he put away the game, Dad said, "This reminds me of the old days when we lived in Merritt. Remember how we used to play crib by candlelight whenever the power went out?"

My throat tightened and I bit my cheeks. It hurt, but it helped keep my emotions in check. "That's in the past, Dad."

"I know I promised we'd go back," he said. "This was meant to be a temporary solution." He put his hand over mine.

I pulled my hand away and immediately felt guilty. Looking at the ground, I mumbled, "It's okay, Dad."

But I didn't believe that. I'd been dealing with our *temporary* situation for six months. With the city clearing the forest beside us for a development, there was a new threat.

What would happen next?

My insides felt tight. I didn't feel like talking anymore. I told my dad I had homework to read for English class and slumped to bed. I pulled the covers around my shoulders, but I couldn't get warm. After reading thirteen pages, I realized none of it was sinking in. My mind was on Inna, the social studies project and the cleared land by our home.

When I finally drifted off to sleep, my dreams were strange. First Inna and I were watching a movie and eating licorice. Then I was at a picnic with my mom and dad in a forest where fiddleheads and cedar trees reached for the sun. Mounds of food covered the picnic blanket. As she offered me a piece of blackberry pie, my mom smiled. Her hair fell over her shoulders like a waterfall.

She leaned in to hug me. But instead of feeling her soft arms, I felt metal clasps, like an oversized Transformer. A machine grabbed me. It whipped me into the air then pulled me out of the forest and left me dangling over a gaping hole in the earth.

Just as the machine released me, I heard a scream and woke up.

Chapter Six

Bulldozers rumbled nearby. Trees crashed to the ground. I pulled myself out of bed and checked on my dad. Amazingly, he was still asleep. Sleeping was something he was good at.

When my mom was alive, we used to get up early. Fridays were the best. Mom didn't work Fridays, so she would make us a big breakfast. Banana pancakes with real maple syrup. Before Dad left for work, he'd give my mom a wet, slurpy kiss.

Now my dad slept most of the day. He had gone from trying to find a job to trying to find money for food. I guess it's hard to get out of bed when you don't have much to look forward to.

Another tree came crashing down. It sounded like it was only a few feet away. I panicked and rushed to my dad's side.

"Dad! Dad…Get up!" I rolled his shoulder back and forth in an attempt to wake him.

He slowly opened his eyes. "What's the trouble, son?"

"I think they're clearing too close. What are we going to do?"

My dad rolled out of his bed and stood on shaky legs. Yawning, he tousled my hair. "It'll be okay, Edgar. They're a good hundred feet away."

I knew my numbers. "A hundred feet is not enough! We need to do something."

"*You* need to go to school. Leave this with me. I'll take care of it," Dad said as he pulled on his pants. He had already made two extra holes in his belt, and it looked like he was going to have to make another one. He used to be strong, but now he was a rack of bones. He looked like an old man.

"Go on. Get to school. Everything will be fine."

I wasn't so sure.

I trudged off to school. Once I was out of the range of workmen and noise, I remembered I'd be seeing Inna. Her smile motivated me up the hill. I ate my muffin but felt a little off-balance after eating.

Once I arrived at school, I headed straight for the office to wait.

Sixteen phone calls and three visitors later, Inna walked through the door.

My heart beating a hundred miles an hour, I rushed out to greet her.

We had a different set of blocks today, so I had to read Inna's schedule again so I'd know where to take her. Outside her room, I pointed to a spot for her to wait so I could guide her to her next class. After each bell, she'd be scrunched up against a locker, biting her nails, her eyes wide, scanning the halls. She smiled with relief when she spotted me. We repeated this routine all morning.

At lunch she agreed to sit with me. Being a tour guide had its perks. We found a spot outside, away from the crowds. I laid my coat on the ground for a blanket.

Inna smiled. "Tsank you." She opened her lunch bag and pulled out a plastic container with cabbage rolls in it. I realized I should have grabbed something from the breakfast program.

I sifted through my backpack and found a mangled-looking granola bar. It would have to do.

"You like?" Inna held out the lid of a plastic container with a cabbage roll on it.

"Cool. Yeah, I like cabbage rolls. How do you say this in your language?"

She wrinkled her nose at me. I tried asking the question again, with my index finger pointing first at the food, then at her. "How would you say this in the Ukraine?"

"Ah. *Holubtsi*. Ho…lub…si."

"Hol…*butt*…si," I tried.

She laughed. "Holubsti. Ya. Is good. Holubtsi. You like?"

I took a bite. I remembered having warm cabbage rolls, but never cold. They tasted great anyway.

Inna smiled as I downed the food way too quickly. She took small bites of her cabbage roll, then placed another one on the lid I was using as a plate.

"Why did you have to go home yesterday?" I said each word slowly, to give her time to absorb the meaning.

"Home." She reached into her backpack and pulled out a piece of crumpled paper. She passed it to me, while rummaging in her pack again.

I read the paper she offered me. It had her street address and phone number scrawled in tiny letters with purple ink. As I stared at the note, she handed me a blank piece of paper and the purple pen.

"You give me...home?" She nodded.

"I...I..." I couldn't think of a response and felt my pulse quicken. My eyes searched the ground for something to focus on.

She took my hand and opened my tight grasp. I had crumpled the sheet in my fist. Inna took the blank paper and replaced it in her bag. Then she put her fingers through mine and leaned her head on my shoulder.

She smelled like a summer picnic, like flowers and watermelon.

I loved that she didn't ask me more questions and pretended nothing happened. I loved that her quiet breathing was so hypnotic.

Twenty-four breaths—in and out. Then the bell rang.

Chapter Seven

In social studies, Mr. Brock began the class by telling us we were going to preview the social justice course. At our school, social justice classes were only for grade eleven and twelve students. As Mr. Brock circulated around the room, he handed various newspaper stories out to each table of students. My table got the story that he'd projected onto the screen yesterday.

I felt my knees wobble.

"I want one member of each group to read the article aloud to your table. Then I want you to talk about what you've read and what it means to you. I hope you understand the importance of what we're discussing today."

Mr. Brock was a blur, and his words just as fuzzy. I kept trying to count the number of branches on the fir outside the window, but I couldn't keep track. "Sean, your table will look at the statistical information, and Kelsey, your group will look at the global picture."

Mr. Brock stopped pacing as he reached our table. He placed his hand on my shoulder. "Edgar, your group will look at our local scene."

I felt like I might black out. I needed to chill.

"Any questions?" Hearing none, Mr. Brock urged us to begin.

My group looked at me. *What? Did Mr. Brock make me the leader when he said my name?* I wasn't about to read the story.

I had managed to keep my secret since the beginning of the school year. I wasn't going to blow it now.

"Well? Aren't you going to read the article?" Janie was eyeing me. Shane looked bored, and Paul was snickering.

"Hey, if one of you wants to read it, I don't care." I hoped someone would bite. It would be easier to get through the next forty minutes if I wasn't the focus of attention. But no one offered to take my place. The knot in my stomach seemed to be reaching up to my throat. I had to swallow several times before I could find my voice.

"Jack, as he likes to be called," I began, the paper rattling in my hands, *"once held a prominent position in a bank, but now likes to keep his numbers simple."*

I looked at the group. No one was really paying attention. Other groups were only half listening to the person reading their article too.

Why couldn't I have been at the table with the stats?

I continued, "*One blanket, one pair of shoes, one picture.*"

"What's the picture of?" asked Janie.

"Dunno," I replied. I scanned the column for an answer, glad for a distraction. "Oh, here it is. It says the picture is of his daughter. According to this article, he hasn't been in contact with her for several years."

Janie shook her head. "Why would anyone do that? Why would they leave their family behind?"

Shane still looked bored. Paul was doodling on his notebook.

"I like the tone of the conversation here," said Mr. Brock as he approached our table. "Are you wondering what causes people to live on the street?"

"Yeah. Laziness. That's all. People like them don't like to work." Paul flipped his book over so Mr. Brock couldn't see the picture.

"Do you all agree with Paul?" Mr. Brock was eyeing me as he waited for someone to answer.

No one was biting.

When would the bell go? Why couldn't he have stuck to the regular curriculum?

"Edgar. Any ideas?"

My days of low profile were over. I couldn't blend into the woodwork anymore. "Well," I started tentatively, "I guess lots of things cause a person to become homeless."

There. I said it.

Homeless.

At least the article wasn't about my dad and me.

Chapter Eight

I could hear Casey saying something about how over 200,000 people could be homeless in Canada on any given night. Mr. Brock and the rest of my group were still looking at me, waiting for me to continue. But I didn't know the answer. I didn't know why other people lived on the streets. I only knew what happened to my dad and me.

"Maybe something bad happens in their life?" I looked at Mr. Brock. He nodded, encouraging me to go on. "Maybe people can't keep a job because they lose someone special to them."

"Then they should see a shrink. They're supposed to help you deal with that crap," snickered Paul.

"*Language*," cautioned Mr. Brock, as he moved toward Kelsey's table.

"What could happen that would be so bad you'd rather live in a dirty alley than sleep in a real bed?" asked Janie.

"I think it's 'cause they're *lazy*," said Shane. "They like living off the government. Then when the government gets wise to their tricks and cuts them off, they become even bigger bums. That's what my dad says."

I pulled at my shirt collar. I tried to count the number of nouns in the article.

"Yeah, but there are *kids* who are homeless," added Janie. "Who would do that? Why wouldn't the parents get a job at McDonald's or something? Then at least they could bring food home."

"You all make it sound so easy. You don't know anything!" My voice was tight and louder than I expected.

"Well, you don't have to go all psycho on us." Paul looked at me like I was an alien.

I closed my eyes, hoping to block them out, but someone laughed. Hot blood raced through my veins. My breath was at the back of my throat, not coming from my chest. A burning energy pulsed into my hands.

"Bottom line is, those kind of people don't count," said Paul. "Besides, half of them are crackheads anyway."

Before I knew what I was doing, I shoved my textbook across the desk into Paul's chest. "Shut up!" I yelled. My hand squeezed into a fist. All I could see was my dad's face as he sent out résumé after résumé. But instead of plowing Paul, I slammed my chair into the floor. "My dad lost his job because he spent every day at the hospital caring for my mom. Do you know what it's like praying someone will offer your fifty-four-year-old dad a job?"

"We didn't know," said Janie. "We didn't mean…"

Janie and Shane exchanged glances. I could feel my cheeks burning with shame. I wondered what they were thinking. Then Mr. Brock returned to our table. If they suspected I was homeless, I hoped they wouldn't say anything to our teacher. All I'd need is for him to call social services. They'd want to see where I live—how could I explain I live in a tent? I'd be put into foster care and never see my dad again.

How would he manage by himself?

"Everything all right here?" asked Mr. Brock.

"Edgar was telling us—," Janie started.

I jumped in. "I was explaining how the man in this article might have ended up on the street. I got angry with Paul for saying that every homeless person is a drug addict. That's just NOT TRUE." Paul glared at me.

"Edgar's right," said Mr. Brock. "People make assumptions about the homeless without knowing the whole story."

Paul shook his head, his mouth curved into a smirk.

I couldn't regulate my breathing. If I stayed another minute, I'd lose it. I wanted to hit Paul. I wanted to make him look the way I felt inside—bruised. "Mr. Brock, can I be excused to go to the washroom?" I asked. Then, without waiting for his answer, I stormed out of the class.

Who was I kidding? Sooner or later someone would find out and report me. How could I ever think I'd get to university?

As I sulked down the hall, I passed Inna's room. She was looking out the window. Her teacher was talking fast, and I'm sure Inna couldn't keep up. Worrying about her helped to take my mind off my problems.

But I still wondered how I would face my classmates after freaking out.

Chapter Nine

The afternoon dragged on. After the last bell, I hung around Inna's class, hoping I'd see her.

I wasn't sure what to say to her when she stepped into the hall. I only knew I needed whatever it was she was giving me…her smile, her hand…I'd take any of it right now.

"Want to see the beach?" I asked, surprised by my suggestion.

She shrugged and tilted her head sideways, her caramel hair draping her arm.

"Water. Sand." I gestured, "Swim."

She laughed. "Too cold…"

"No, not to swim. I mean, yeah, it's too cold to swim. We can just walk." I tried mimicking the actions again, hoping she understood. I wished now I'd played charades more often when my mom was alive. She loved that game.

"Yah. We go for walk at bich." I laughed at her accent. Then I felt badly because she didn't know why I was laughing. I wanted her to feel comfortable trying to speak, so I apologized. She smiled and took my hand.

Once at the bus stop, all I could think about was how I was going to pay for this "date" I'd decided to go on.

I rifled through my pockets to see how much change I had while Inna texted her parents. Dad had given me a few bucks for lunch. Since I'd eaten with Inna, I had enough for bus fare and one coffee or ice cream.

After a short ride, we got off on Marine Drive and strolled along the pier. Inna kept her hand in mine.

Two eagles circled overhead before they flew off toward the trees. Sailboats rocked in their berths at the end of the pier. Inna used her cell phone to take a picture of a seagull with a starfish in its beak.

I knew she didn't understand much English, so maybe that's what got me started. Or maybe it was the warmth of her soft fingers intertwined with mine? Whatever it was, I found myself blabbing my life story to her.

As we left the pier and walked toward the big white rock the city is named for, I said, "You know earlier today? I didn't mean to get all strange about my address. You see, the truth is, I don't have an address. No address. No phone number. I actually live in a tent. With my dad. In the trees. We're in a small patch of forest between a shopping plaza and the street. Can you believe that?"

I chanced a look her way. Her eyes were on a couple sitting on the bench to the side of us. They were kissing. I figured it was safe to continue. Inna wasn't really paying attention, and I don't think she caught all of what I was saying. I must have needed to tell my story even if Inna didn't understand all of the words.

"The problem is," I said, speaking quickly, "the city has decided to build more townhouses. Like we don't have enough already. So I'm worried they're going to spot us. I don't know what to do. I could maybe live with Ben…for a while, but then what about my dad?"

"Dad?" That got Inna's attention. "You have mom and dad, no?"

"I…I have a dad, yeah. But, my mom…died…last spring. Cancer." I didn't know if that word translated, but she seemed to understand.

"Cancer and my grandma. She dead. Two months."

"You *just* lost your grandma? That's really sad," I said. "I still cry sometimes when I think of my mom. Mostly I miss her laugh. And the way she made me feel better when things were crappy. You know how moms do that?"

Inna didn't respond. Instead she said, "I have mom and dad and tree brudders. You have brudders or seesters?"

I used to be so happy I was an only child. I got all of my parents' attention and never had to share anything. Now I wished I had a sibling to help me out, or at least, to keep me company. Doing this solo was really tough. "Just me," I answered, leading us back toward the main strip.

I bought Inna a coffee at a shop on the corner. I felt lighter after talking about the stuff that was stressing me out. As the temperature dropped and rain began to fall, I thought we'd better head home.

Inna drank her coffee while we waited for the bus. After a few sips, she shared the cup with me. Wind ripped through our jackets, and Inna shivered. To help keep her warm, I draped my coat around her shoulders. Black clouds filled the sky.

As the bus drove up the hill toward the school, tennis balls of hail bounced off the roof.

Chapter Ten

I said goodbye to Inna at the bus stop, then raced down the hill. Panic pushed my body into overdrive. Hail dropped into the space between my jacket and my neck, sending an icy chill down my spine. Even before I reached our site, I could see the damage.

The wind had knocked down several small trees, and now the orange and blue tarps covering our tent could be seen from the street. A plastic bag flew past me like tumbleweed. If we didn't secure the tarps, they'd be next. My dad was running around the campsite tying things down and putting loose items under cover. We didn't have much, so we couldn't afford to lose anything to a storm.

"This came up fast," my dad hollered as I approached. "Grab my bike, will you, son?"

"Sure, Dad." I pushed the bicycle toward my father. He rolled it inside our tent. Hail covered the ground like Styrofoam. A squirrel raced up the tree beside me, looking for shelter.

"What are we going to do, Dad? This is the worst storm I've ever seen. Look at the trees falling. There's no way we can hide our site now."

"We'll get through tonight and consider our options in the morning.

Once we have everything tied down, we can head to the coffee shop and have…"

"What?" My dad's voice was lost to the wind. He gestured toward the small camping table. I quickly turned it on its side and folded the legs, then pushed it into the tent to help hold it down.

There would be no room for us once we loaded everything inside. I don't think my dad was too concerned.

A crack of thunder made me jump. The wind wasn't letting up. My eyes stung, and my lungs wheezed with each breath. My dad was hunched over, gathering pots and pans into his sweater.

I pulled extra rope through the holes of the two tarps. On the last hole, the wind whipped the tarp, and the rope tore from my hands, burning my flesh. I grimaced with pain but grabbed the swinging rope and wrapped it around the nearest tree. I tied three knots, hoping they would hold.

Snap! Crack!

An alder branch split and careened down on my dad's head. He fell sideways. His face scrunched up with pain as he hit the ground.

"Dad!" I yelled, running to his side. "Are you okay?"

"I may have broken my arm." He looked pale.

"Let's get out of here, Dad. I don't care if we lose everything. All that matters is that you're all right." He stumbled as I helped him up.

"I'm fine. I just need some food. Grab our winter coats, will you?"

I put my dad's jacket over his shoulders and guided him toward the street. It was going to be a long walk to the hospital. Then I remembered the clinic down by the freeway.

I took one last look at our site. Most of our stuff was in the tent. I'd closed the flap on my way out. I could only hope that it would be there tomorrow.

Then I remembered something I couldn't afford to leave behind.

"Dad, stand here for a minute, okay?" I ran back to the tent. I rummaged through our stuff. The wind rumbled through the thin walls and seemed to want to lift me off the ground.

I found what I was looking for. I put it under my hoodie, tied the tent flap down again and ran back to take my dad's good arm.

Bending my head down, we moved into the headwind. When we reached the coffee shop, my dad tugged on my sleeve.

"We're here, son. This is as far as I can go…I need to sit down."

"But, Dad," I protested. "Shouldn't we go to the clinic? Get you some help?"

He sighed. "I let our health-care payments lapse. They'd want to know our address. I'd have to tell them our situation, fill in forms. I honestly don't have the energy for that right now." He pulled away from my grasp. "Just let me rest. I'm tired."

"But…"

He staggered toward the door.

"Dad!" I called after him.

Ignoring me, he opened the door and entered the coffee shop.

Chapter Eleven

Warm air and the aroma of fresh coffee and chicken soup greeted me as I entered. My dad was already seated at a table in the back. This was the best spot, because it was out of the staff's range of vision. There was a video camera hoisted above us, but I was pretty sure nobody watched it. I didn't want anyone kicking us out tonight. We had nowhere to go.

"Okay, Dad. We'll stay here. But you need some food." I rummaged through my backpack.

"Do you have any money?" he asked.

I hesitated. I was embarrassed to tell my dad I'd spent the last of our money on a girl. I shook my head.

"Well, I don't have any. I was so busy trying to find a new spot to pitch our tent that I didn't have time to hunt for bottles."

He looked so hungry. Pain flashed across his face as he leaned on his injured arm.

I lied: "I just remembered, Dad. I left the cash at the site." Looking at the floor, I said, "I'll go back and get it."

"I'm not that hungry, Edgar. Stay inside. Stay warm."

I ignored him and started toward the door. "Wait here," I said over my shoulder. "I'll be right back."

I left my dad slumped at the table. The air that hit me as I opened the door felt twenty degrees colder than inside. The blue awning offered some cover, but it shook on its hinges with each gust of wind. I wasn't sure the awning would hold, so I moved to where the sidewalk was exposed to the storm.

A lady bundled in a scarf was coming toward the door. I'd never panhandled before, but tonight I had no choice. I mumbled, "Excuse me, ma'am. Could you spare some change?" Either she didn't hear me or didn't want to help. She brushed past me and entered the coffee shop.

This was going to be tough!

Moving to the side of the building got me out of my dad's range of vision. He'd flip if he saw me asking for a handout.

He always said we would earn our way, even if that meant collecting bottles or returning grocery carts. But there was no time for that right now. I had to find another way. Dad was counting on me.

Another lady approached the door. *Come on*, I said to myself. *You can do this*. As she passed me, I forced my head up. "Sorry to bother you," my breath was shallow as I talked. "Is there any chance you could help me out?" I turned my palms up and looked at the ground again.

"You poor child. It's freezing out here," she replied.

"If you have some spare…"

"Of course, dear. You get inside now and warm up." She dropped a couple of dollars into my open hand.

Since that wasn't enough, I didn't follow her inside.

Other than the howling wind, it was quiet. I rubbed my hands together to stay warm. My jacket offered little protection from the frigid cold. After what seemed like an eternity, a man and his wife left the fancy restaurant a few doors down. The wind caught his jacket, blowing it open to show his gray suit. As I approached them, I pushed my pride aside and worked the helpless-kid angle. I must have done it well, because he gave up a crisp five-dollar bill.

Bingo!

Now we could get some food.

Back in the coffee shop, I ordered my dad soup and tea, and a muffin and coffee for myself. I figured I'd better hang on to the rest of the cash so I could stay awake all night. I was going to need a lot of caffeine!

"Oh, that tasted good," said my dad, while I nibbled on my muffin. "I guess I worked up an appetite during the storm." He slurped the last of his soup and wiped his unshaven chin with a napkin. Bits of the napkin stuck to the bristle.

"Ah, Dad." I gestured to his chin. He wiped them away with the back of his hand.

"Aargh." He grimaced.

He'd used his sore arm. It looked swollen. I should have grabbed a scarf from our tent to make a sling for him. I looked through the stuff I had with me to see what I could use.

"Here, Dad, take my jacket. We'll use my sleeve to hold your arm up." It took a few minutes, but I was able to turn my coat into a makeshift sling.

"That's better," my dad sighed. He leaned his head back against the wall and rested.

I picked at my muffin and watched the people in the restaurant. There were lots of kids with their parents, picking up meals to take home for the evening.

"So, I did look around today for a place to stay," Dad said after a while. "Good timing, hey? I tried the shelters again. No change there."

"What else is new?" I said.

"I'd really hoped I could give you good news. I never meant to let you down…"

"Dad, it's okay. Right now, let's focus on you getting better."

"Yeah. I guess. Listen, I rode out toward Langley, and I found us a spot where we won't be noticed. There's only one problem."

I couldn't imagine anything worse than the situation we were in. Whatever my dad had planned had to be better than this.

"What is it?" I asked.

"Well, I don't think you'll like this part. But I don't know what else to do. We have to move, and we have to move now. The place I found is nowhere near your school, or any school, for that matter.

You'll have to catch a bus and attend a high school in Langley."

Ordinarily, this wouldn't have bothered me. But I liked the classes this school offered.

Besides, Ben's my best buddy, and I'd just met Inna.

I couldn't change schools now.

Chapter Twelve

Finally my dad slept, snoring every few moments. I checked on the staff behind the counter. They were too busy gabbing with each other to notice us. I figured it would be safe to go wash. I wanted to get cleaned up before it got busy in the coffee shop. Besides, I was tired of counting how many times the younger staff said, "*Like*."

I always have supplies in my backpack. I usually showered and shampooed at school on pe days. When I didn't have gym, I used this washroom or the one at McDonald's. Both had a handicapped space that was private. I could sponge-bathe and wash my hair in the sink. I barely needed to shave, so I didn't have to worry about that every day. I usually brushed my teeth at our site, but today I did everything here.

Just as I was finishing up, the door handle turned.

"It's busy," I said. I always stressed when someone needed to use the washroom, like I'd be found out. I finished cleaning up, put on fresh underwear and a clean shirt, then stuffed everything back into my backpack.

When I returned to the table, my dad was awake and looking out the window.

"Hey, Dad. How does your arm feel this morning?"

"Not bad at all," he lied.

He looked like he was in a ton of pain. Even Tylenol would help. I'd have to scrounge for bottles to buy a pain-killer. Then I had a brainwave.

"Dad, I have to go to school soon. Do you think you'll be okay here?"

"Oh, sure. I may even head back to the campsite to check out the damage. Hopefully, we didn't lose too much."

"Yeah," I said, "I think we did a good job of tying things down. I'm sure it will be fine. I can walk with you to our site."

"No. It's easier to go straight to school from here. Why don't you head off? We'll meet this afternoon and then figure out a plan."

We parted at the door, and, after making sure my dad was steady on his feet, I ran up the hill to school. I probably beat my old record—the caffeine made me hyper. I actually had a bit of a headache when I got to school.

I figured that would make what I was about to do easier.

I headed straight for the office. Mr. Brock was at the photocopy machine when I opened the office door.

"Hi, Mr. Brock," I said, trying to squint so it looked like my head was really hurting.

"How are you today, Edgar? I was concerned when you left class yesterday. You seemed frustrated."

"Oh, yeah—I was ticked with Paul. It's all cool now. But," I said, rubbing my temples for effect, "I do have a migraine. I get them around exams when I'm up late reading. Any chance the medical room has some Tylenol?"

"Oh, I'm sure they do. But I'm not allowed to dispense it to students. Let me see if Mr. Johnson is around. Just hang on, okay?"

"Sure. Thanks." I watched him head toward the library and spotted Ben coming in the front doors. He was early today too.

"Poe...dude. I'm glad you're here. You won't believe what I heard on the news." He jerked his head sideways, like he wanted me to come into the hall.

"Just a sec. I'm waiting for Mr. Brock." Ben approached the counter and leaned against it. He looked agitated. I was starting to wonder what had him so riled up when Mr. Brock returned.

"Here, hopefully these will help. Maybe you should get your eyes tested." He discreetly placed the two pills in my hand and then patted my shoulder.

"Thanks. I'm sure these will do the trick. I just have to get some water." I moved out to the hall, where there was a drinking fountain. Ben followed, and Mr. Brock returned to his photocopying. I pretended to swallow the Tylenol in case any adults were watching. Then I placed them in my pants pocket. I would have to skip classes to get them to my dad. The way he looked when we left the coffee shop, I didn't think he'd last until 3:00 PM. Besides, all I could think about was our site and the damage the storm might have done.

"So, what were you going to tell me?" I asked Ben as we moved toward our lockers.

"Dude, it was all over the news today."

"Hang on," I said. "Why are you here so early?"

"I thought if I got here early, you could help me with math."

"I guess," I said. "But I don't plan on staying long." I didn't have the headspace for this right now, but Ben seemed to really need my help. I pulled my texts from my locker.

"Forget the math," Ben said. "It doesn't matter anymore. This is big. I mean, really big." His voice had tensed, and his eyes were wild-looking.

"Okay, what's wrong?" I asked, feeling my nerves heat up.

"Mom had the radio on when she drove me to school. They were saying the storm knocked out power last night and took down trees."

"So, tell me something I don't know," I said. I closed my locker and began to walk down the hall.

"A bunch of trees in that forested area at the bottom of the hill came down. They found a campsite, and they think some homeless guy was living there. They figure he had a kid too, from the clothes they found. The police are there now."

Everything went fuzzy.

My dad and I had been discovered.

Chapter Thirteen

My head was really pounding now. I looked around, but no one was watching us. What did it matter, anyway? My secret was out. If the police were at our site, they probably had my dad in custody.

"You knew I was living in a tent?" I asked Ben.

"It *was* you!" he replied.

"What! You mean you didn't know?" I felt a burn behind my eyes and blinked hard. "Why'd you trick me like that? I thought we were friends." I turned to leave, but he pulled on my shirt, so I sat down.

"Relax. I suspected it was you as soon as I heard the news. You've never had me to your place, and you're always hard up for food. I figured you and your dad were just tight for cash. I didn't know until today that things were *that* bad for you."

My breathing was shallow, and every breath made my head hurt more.

"Listen, Poe. I really didn't know. I would have helped," he said, sitting down beside me. "You *could* stay with me. My folks won't mind."

"Yeah. Well, thanks for the offer, but that doesn't really help my dad, does it?" I don't know why I was giving Ben attitude. He was the only friend I had, and right now I needed support. "Sorry," I said, then put my head between my knees.

Suddenly the lack of sleep hit me and I felt exhausted. "Right now there's only one thing on my mind. I have to find my dad." I stood up to leave. "I think he broke his arm yesterday, and I don't know if he got hauled in by the cops or what."

Ben stood up too. "I'm coming with you."

I had no energy to argue, and frankly, I think I needed Ben. I wasn't steady on my feet. "I'm really sorry I snapped."

"Hey, no worries, dude. I can't imagine how you've been living in a tent all this time…and through the winter? Man, you and your dad must be strong. I couldn't do that."

As we walked out the doors, I saw Inna leaving her parents' car. She bent in to kiss her mom goodbye, then waved at Ben and me.

What would I tell her?

Inna's parents were eyeing us from their car. I waved, hoping they'd be satisfied and drive off. But they continued staring. As she reached us, Inna grabbed my arm and practically pulled it out of the socket, dragging me into the school foyer.

"No...hi...I mean. Let *go*," I said, trying to pry her hand loose. She looked hurt. "I'm sorry, Inna. But Ben and I have to go. Leave...goodbye."

I guess tact goes out the window when you haven't slept all night.

She shook her head and put her arms up to signify she didn't know what I was talking about. I didn't know what to do. But I couldn't be in the building another minute.

"Goodbye," she finally stated, when I didn't say anything. Then she stomped down the hall.

"Well, that went well," said Ben.

"Shut it," I said back.

"Hey, I'm on your side, remember?"

"Now I've screwed up with Inna too. She's the best thing that ever happened to me."

"Dude, she'll come around. The timing was bad, that's all. But we better get going before the bell rings and a teacher nabs us."

"How are we going to find my dad?" I asked as we stepped into the crisp air again.

"Let's find a coffee shop with a TV and check the news. Maybe they'll say if your dad is in custody."

Custody. There was that word again. It sounded scary. Dangerous.

Could they put my dad in jail? Could they lock him up for living with his kid this way? I wished I'd never left him alone this morning. I felt the two painkillers in my pocket. A lot of good they'd do him now. I took a deep breath and felt my temples burn. "Good idea," I replied to Ben's suggestion. Then I downed the two pills, dry.

As we walked, Ben filled the silence. "You know," he said, "you've got to look at this like one of those Greek tragedies. The kind where the hero undergoes a bunch of trials. Fights off three-headed dogs and comes out triumphant."

"Right," I smirked. "It's called a *tragedy* for a reason."

"Okay. But at least he gets the girl in the end." Ben didn't sound convinced.

It was over nine hundred steps to the coffee shop. I lost track on account of the pain in my head.

"*In local news*," a woman on TV said, "*a homeless man was discovered near the remnants of his tent after last night's storm ripped through his home. It appears the man's son was living with him.*

Authorities found clothing and school-books at the site. The man has been taken to the Peace Arch Hospital for medical attention..."

Without waiting to hear the rest of the story, I turned to Ben and said, "Let's go!" It would take a good twenty minutes to get to the hospital, even if we hustled.

Now I knew that my dad's arm was being taken care of. That was good. Our secret was out, so I didn't have to lie anymore. That was good. But what would happen to us?

That's what scared me now.

Chapter Fourteen

The Tylenol was kicking in as we arrived at the hospital, so my head felt better. But my stomach was churning. Ben got us a chocolate bar from a vending machine, and then we followed the signs to the emergency room.

A crew of reporters was in the waiting area as we came around the corner. Ben eyed them suspiciously while I went to the counter to ask about my dad. Even though I used a really low voice, the cameraman beside me yelled, "This must be the kid!"

I turned to run. Ben put himself between the news people and me. In an instant, I realized that if I ran, I'd have to stay on the run. They knew my dad had a kid. It would only be a matter of time before they tracked me down. I didn't want that. All I wanted was for my dad to be okay.

"Are you Mr. Reed's son?" a woman asked as she shoved a microphone into my face.

Maybe it was the lack of food. Maybe it was the knowledge that we'd just lost everything. Or maybe it was because the worst had already happened. Whatever it was, I decided to be honest.

"Yeah. I'm his son," I answered.

"So you were living in a *tent* with your dad? How long has this been going on?" she asked in an accusatory tone.

"You don't want to hear about last night? How my dad broke his arm? How we lost everything we own? Does it matter where we were sleeping? Shouldn't the real question be, where are we going to sleep tonight?"

"Yes, but you didn't answer me," she replied, looking into the camera. "*Why* were you living in a tent and how long were the two of you in the woods?"

"My dad didn't plan this, you know. It's not like he wanted to live in a tent. He had a good job when we lived in Merritt, and we had a home. Bad stuff happens. Maybe if someone had hired my dad after my mom died, we would have been okay." I saw Ben nod and smile, encouraging me to go on.

"But why didn't you stay in a shelter?" asked the reporter.

I was on a roll now. "In Surrey and White Rock, there aren't any shelters that take men *and* their kids. There are shelters for women and kids. There are shelters for men by themselves. And for teenagers, you can maybe find shelter in Vancouver. If you're lucky," I said. "But my dad and I don't want to be separated. He wants to help me with my homework. He wants to be there for me." I could feel a lump forming in my throat. "This wasn't supposed to happen."

"So you're saying there's a gap in the services?" she asked.

"You bet there is," I replied.

"Even so, you could have reached out to social services," she added.

"So I could go into foster care? No way! My dad and I want to stay together. And we were doing all right. That is, until the city started clear-cutting and the storm destroyed our site."

My shoulders relaxed a little. Out of the corner of my eye, I saw Ben clapping. I managed a smile.

"Can I just see my dad? I want to make sure he's okay." Tears threatened to well up into my eyes.

"I'm Sandra Kelley, reporting live from White Rock," she said. Then she gave the cameraman a signal to stop filming. "Hey, kid, you did a good thing. The camera loves your face, and a lot of people are going to be touched by your story. Sorry I pushed."

I returned to the emergency desk. Making Ms. Kelley feel better wasn't high on my list of priorities. The nurse had my dad's information ready. "He's been moved to a room upstairs for the day," she said.

"He's okay, isn't he?" I asked.

"I'm sure he is. Room four-twenty-two." She pointed to the elevator.

"Thanks," I said, then turned to Ben. "Let's go."

My stomach jumped as the elevator landed on my dad's floor. I needed something more in my belly. The chocolate bar wasn't cutting it.

Trays of food were going by as we walked down the hall. Ben saw me eyeing the breakfast items.

"I'll go to the cafeteria and get you something. What do you want?" he asked.

"It's okay."

"No, I'm serious. You need food. Besides, it'll give you and your dad a few minutes on your own. Really, dude." He shook his head. "You need to eat. You're as gray as the hospital gowns."

Chapter Fifteen

Dad was sitting up in bed when I entered his room. His cheeks had some color, and he looked rested. His arm was in a blue cast.

"Nice color, Dad."

"Who knew? I've never seen casts like this before. Pretty classy-looking, hey?"

I smiled and sat down on the edge of his bed.

"How come they're keeping you here if it's just a broken arm?"

"Oh, I guess they're worried I'm a little anemic. They're pumping me full of vitamins. To be truthful, the bed feels great." He patted the empty space beside him, and I climbed up.

It felt like heaven. I knew if I closed my eyes, I'd be gone for sure.

"Edgar, I'm so sorry about all of this. We lost everything. A city crew was cleaning up our belongings when I arrived. I lost my temper and started yelling at them. Guess that's how I ended up here."

"It's okay, Dad."

"What upsets me most is how this is going to impact you," he added. "I don't know what to say."

"Dad, I think I already said it all. On the news. I was interviewed downstairs. I told the truth. Whatever happens now, well…"

My dad tousled my hair. "My son, the TV star!"

I wish it were that easy. I wish I'd been interviewed for any other reason than this. Dad must have sensed my worry.

"Listen, Edgar. I guess the doctors feel that I am suffering from depression. Some days I could see how bad it was, but most days I was just going through the motions. I kept hoping things would get better. But the more we lost, I guess the harder it was to stay positive. I really let you down."

I was about to answer when Ben came into the room with a tray of food. I was glad for the distraction. I also hoped this meant my dad would now be able to get back on his feet. While I ate, Ben and my dad talked.

"If it weren't for the weather, it could be kind of cool camping out every night," said Ben. "Except it would be more fun with a campfire for roasting marshmallows."

"Well, I think if you were to ask Edgar, he'd say the novelty of camping wore off pretty fast. Especially with the first rain." A nurse came in and checked my dad's pulse.

"He's okay, right?" I asked.

"Yes, he's just fine. A couple of meals and a good rest, and he'll be raring to go."

"When can he return home?" I asked, wincing as I said the word *home*.

"The doctor has only given orders for him to stay one night. He can check out in the morning." Then the nurse moved to help the patient in the bed opposite my dad. The old woman was in a cast that went from her chest to her toes.

"Mr. Reed," started Ben, "Poe can stay with me if he wants. I mean, if that's okay with you. I know my parents will be cool with that. Hey, they'll probably be okay with you staying too. We have an extra room downstairs. It's not completely finished, but it's got to be better than living out…"

"Thank you, Ben. I'm sure *Poe* and I will work something out." He yawned, and I realized he needed to rest.

I gave him a hug, and Ben and I headed down the hall to the elevator. Once we were outside, the weight of everything that had happened sat like an elephant on my shoulders.

At least I'd have a place to sleep for the night. Maybe with a good rest, my dad and I would figure something out.

Back at school they were already on the last block before lunch. Ben and I hung around outside, waiting for the bell to ring.

My TV debut hadn't aired yet, and even if it had, everyone was in class, so they wouldn't have seen it. Tomorrow, I'd have to worry.

I didn't see Inna over the lunch hour, nor did I spot her during afternoon classes. When the bell finally rang, I could hardly wait to get to Ben's house. All I could think about was sleeping. For a year!

His mom made meatloaf and mashed potatoes for supper. My dad would have loved this. Ben's parents were really cool about what happened. They didn't ask questions or anything. The conversation stuck to our classes and exams and what we'd be taking next year.

Once under the covers, I should have fallen asleep right away. But I still had a lot on my mind. I reached over the side of the bed into my backpack and pulled out the photo album I'd salvaged from our site.

Pictures of my dad, my mom and me filled the pages—pictures of our life before.

I missed that time. I missed my mom. My fingers ran across photos of her the last Christmas we all shared together. Her smile lit up the page. It reminded me of Inna.

Funny how something great, like meeting a cool girl, can happen at the same time as the absolute worst thing in your life.

Before I closed my eyes, I decided I'd ask Ben to borrow his computer in the morning. I had an important message to share with Inna. I only had to find a site that translated my words into her language. Hopefully, she'd still give me a chance.

Chapter Sixteen

Ben let me use his computer, and I translated the message for Inna at the Babel Fish site. Ben's mom made us a breakfast of sausages, eggs, hashbrowns and toast. She made us a great lunch too.

I could get used to this!

At school, I searched for Inna as soon as we arrived. She was waiting outside the front door.

"I'm sorry about yesterday," I started.

She put her fingers to her mouth to indicate I should be quiet. Then she kissed me on the cheek. I hadn't even given her the note yet.

Did this mean I was forgiven?

"My mom, she...TV...saw you..." She seemed to be searching for the words.

"Watched TV?" I asked.

"Yah. She washed the TV. You...on TV...important. Say good things." Inna smiled.

I guess her mom and dad knew some English. I handed Inna the note anyway and watched her face as she scanned the page. A couple of times she wrinkled her nose, so I must have messed up the words. But she seemed to get the general idea, because she kissed me on the cheek again.

There was no way I was moving to Langley now!

Ben, Inna and I hung out until the bell for first class. Even though I was glad the truth was finally out, I was nervous about seeing my classmates. How would they react? I thought of skipping class and hanging in the library. But there were still four months left of school, so that would be a lot of hiding. I decided to face them.

Strangely, no one said anything in the first blocks. They still looked at me the same way they did before I was interviewed. Social studies was after lunch. I figured *that* class would probably be another story.

At lunch, I was on my way to see Inna when Mr. Johnson approached me.

"Mr. Reed. Could you step into my office, please?"

I had been so focused on what the kids at school would think that I hadn't considered the adult reactions to my situation. My shoulders slumped as I followed Mr. Johnson.

My dad, Mrs. Bailey, Mr. Brock and some lady I didn't recognize were all in the room waiting. The elephant from last night tightened its trunk around my waist as I sat down in the empty seat.

"Mr. Reed," began Mr. Johnson. My dad and I said yes at the same time. Mr. Brock smiled, and I relaxed a little.

My principal continued, "I understand you and your father have fallen on rather tough times recently. Mr. Brock says you are a fine student. With all that has happened to you, it is surprising that you've maintained good grades."

Mr. Brock interrupted, "I hope you don't mind me sitting in, Edgar. After I heard the news, well, I wanted to do whatever I could to help out."

I nodded. My dad smiled in Mr. Brock's direction.

Mr. Johnson continued, "Mrs. Munro is with the Ministry of Social Services. She would like to say a few words."

My dad took a deep breath. This lady could hand down a sentence that neither of us wanted.

"In light of the fact that you will be sixteen in three months," she said to me, "and as a family has come forward to sponsor you, I can't see any reason to change your status."

"Who came forward?" My dad and I asked at the same time.

"It seems you have two options. A family named Oleksienko offered to have you stay with them. They suggested you could help their daughter learn to speak English. Also, the Corbin family would be willing to take you in. Apparently they have a son you know. Ben?"

Wow. Two options. They both would be great. Especially after breakfast this morning. I realized now how hungry I've been for the last six months. I looked at my dad. He nodded his head.

"Son, I think this can work. Mrs. Munro has suggested some programs to help me find work. I can stay at the Salvation Army shelter until I get on my feet again. Then you and I can find a low-cost place to stay. Heck, there are some nice campgrounds on Eighth Avenue. Mrs. Munro was telling me the bus goes there every morning to pick up students for school. Your school! I qualify for financial assistance. That will help us get organized sooner."

"I have an old tent trailer," added Mr. Brock. "You are more than welcome to borrow it."

Dry clothes. No more musty smell. Food in my belly. A real bed to sleep on.

Well, at least for a while. Then my dad and I could work our way back. It wouldn't be like it was when my mom was alive, but we would be a family.

The two of us.

And I secretly hoped Inna would take a *loooong* time to learn English.

Acknowledgments

Special thanks to my mom, who instilled in me a love of reading, and to my dad, who encouraged me to dream I could be a writer; both of you helped this story along its journey. Thanks, Lise, for being my sis, and Sean, for continuing to be an inspiration. Thanks also to my editor, Melanie.

Cristy Watson is a teacher who loves reading and writing poetry and YA novels. *Living Rough* is her second entry in the Orca Currents series. Cristy lives in White Rock, British Columbia.

orca currents

The following is an excerpt from
another exciting Orca Currents novel,
Benched by Cristy Watson.

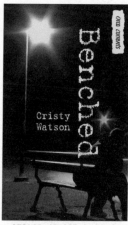

9781554694082 $9.95 pb

When Cody and his friends accept a challenge
from a local gang to steal a park bench, their main
concern is keeping themselves on the gang's good
side. Cody learns that the stolen bench had been
dedicated to the father of the English teacher who
sponsors the school newspaper—the paper that
Cody has just started writing for—and he's worried
about the consequences. As the gang applies
pressure for more from Cody and his friends, he
realizes they've crossed a line, and now he has to
figure out how to make it right.

Chapter One

"About time, Cody." Taz had the volume cranked on his iPod. I could hear Snow Patrol screaming out their latest tune. "Where were you?"

"You're not going to believe who I was just talking to," I said as I struggled to catch my breath.

Bowman scanned the parking lot outside our high school. "Cathy?

That grade eleven you're into?"

"You mean *Cassie*?" I asked. I don't know why Bowman had trouble with her name. "I can handle Cassie. This was... well, strange."

By then Taz was already halfway to the park, our shortcut home. He was almost six feet tall and all legs. Bowman and I had to jog to keep up with him.

"I'm listening," Bowman said.

I looked over my shoulder to make sure no one was following us, and then I lowered my voice. "So I'm leaving the school, and there's this dude leaning against the bike rack, *waiting* for me. He looked familiar, like maybe he used to hang with Dylan."

A lump the size of a grapefruit formed in my throat.

Taz interrupted, "You mean someone from Beaker's gang?"

"Yeah, but I don't know his name," I said.

"What did he want?" asked Bowman. His voice sounded tight.

I hesitated before answering. Should I tell them?

Maybe I could ignore the whole thing, like it didn't happen. But knowing Taz, he wouldn't let this go. Not until he had all the details.

As we neared the west pond, I saw two guys walking our way. I couldn't tell if they were from Beaker's gang. If they were, I wasn't ready to deal with them. Not yet. Not until we decided what to do.

"So, what's up with the dude?" Bowman asked as he bent down to tie his shoelace.

The two guys were coming straight for us. Now that they were closer, I recognized the ballcap one of them was wearing. They were definitely from Beaker's gang.

"I think…what if…," I stammered, "we get an ice cream?" I felt dumb as soon as I said it. "I'll even pay." I hoped Taz and Bowman couldn't tell my nerves were heating up.

"Did someone say Blizzard?" asked Taz. "I'm in!"

Great. That would be the end of my cash, and I'd be broke for the weekend. Again. But it would mean we'd be heading away from Beaker's brutes.

"Like you ever turn down free food," said Bowman, yanking out Taz's earbuds. Taz gave him a look, but Bowman just laughed.

The Dairy Queen was only a block from our school. As we turned around, I glanced over my shoulder. I could still see the two guys. They weren't as tall as Taz, but they were chunky like Bowman. They were way bigger than me. When they saw we'd changed our route, they did the same.

In minutes we were at the restaurant. I was about to tell Taz and Bowman that Beaker's boys were behind us, but the two guys stayed on the sidewalk instead of following us inside. The one with the blue Mohawk leaned against the window and watched us through the glass.

A cold draft rippled down my neck.

We had barely sat down when Bowman started in on me. "Are you gonna finish telling us what that guy wanted?"

"Okay." I leaned in. "So, this dude asks me if I'm Dylan Manning's brother. When I say yeah, he tells me that Beaker wants to see us—the three of us. Like he knows we hang out."

"What do you mean, he wants to *see* us?" Taz sat up and scanned the restaurant.

"I don't know exactly." I poked at my sundae with my spoon, but I didn't take a bite. "He asked if we want to earn some quick cash."

"Go on," said Taz. He looked more interested than worried.

"I think he has some kind of job for us," I said.

"So, what are we waiting for? Let's go find him," said Taz, already out of his seat.

Bowman grabbed his arm. "Hang on. We gotta figure this out. You don't mess around with these guys."

"You've got a point," I said. "So how about we just…skip it?"

The gang had been cool with my brother. That didn't mean they'd be cool with us. They didn't make a habit of hanging out with grade nines. Dylan had never wanted me around, so what did Beaker and his gang want with us?

"Yeah," said Bowman. "But we can't blow them off. They'll think we're dissing them. Besides, I *am* into earning some cash. Maybe we should check out what they want before we decide. Aren't you always saying you're broke?"

I nodded.

"Then what are we waiting for?" asked Taz.

My gut said this was a bad idea. So I don't know why I said, "The dude wants to meet at nine tonight in the park."

"Then let's make sure we're not late," said Bowman.

By the time we were ready to head home, the gang guys were gone. But I had this rumble in the pit of my stomach, and I kept looking over my shoulder as we walked through the park. A sharp bite of wind followed us.

I just wanted the meeting to be over.

orca *currents*

For more information on all the books
in the Orca Currents series, please visit
www.orcabook.com